Little Twig's
Big Adventures

Written by
Lisa Alekna

Illustrated by
Charlotte Watkins

For my boys Will & Oli,
who make me so proud and
helped Twig become the
little legend he is today.

Published in the United Kingdom by:

Blue Falcon Publishing
The Mill, Pury Hill Business Park,
Alderton Road, Towcester
Northamptonshire NN12 7LS
Email: books@bluefalconpublishing.co.uk
Web: www.bluefalconpublishing.co.uk

A CIP record of this book is available from the British Library.

First printed November 2021
ISBN 9781912765386

Little Twig's

Big Adventures

Lisa Alekna

Meet Little Twig, so tiny and weak.
Everyone said that his future was bleak.
The other lambs teased him for being so small,
And were too fast for Twig to play with them all.

He didn't like eating the grass all day long,
And being with sheep quite simply felt wrong!

The only time Twig wasn't lonely and glum
Was during the visits from his shepherd mum.
He longed for his shepherd and her sheepdog, too,
And dreamed of the sofa to sleep on and chew.

Now, Twig had a power like no other lamb.
He could squeeze through the smallest of holes with a plan,
To find his mum shepherd where he must belong,
To cuddle and follow around all day long.

So every day when the shepherd had gone,

A hole Twig would find and his mission was on.

A sniff in the air, a glance at the sun,

"She must have gone this way," and off he would run.

Twig wasn't tiny when out and about.
He'd pass Valerie vole with her very long snout,
Wave to Freddy frog, chat with Miss mole,
And tell them about his escape through the hole.

He passed by Sid snail, gave a nod to each bird,
Who all thought that Twig's plan was simply absurd!
Twig would keep trotting, beaming with pride,
Knowing that he'd soon be back by her side.

Meanwhile the shepherd received a phone call;
Reports of a lamb on the loose that's so small!
The sheepdog and shepherd ran out of the door,
To find their friend Twig and save him once more.

Twig's big adventure had picked up in pace,
Wearing the happiest smile on his face.
Twig was excited, it wouldn't be long.
His mission "Find shepherd" had never gone wrong.

And true to Twig's instinct, there standing tall
Were shepherd and sheepdog; "Twig," they both call.
They scooped up their friend Twig and cuddled with glee,
Confirming Twig's thoughts of how life should be.

Twig's mission at last, accomplished once more,
He trotted in behind them through the farm door.
Curled up on the sofa Twig started to dream
Of what a fabulous day this had been.

The other lambs started to notice Twig go,
Returning each time with the shepherd in tow.

One day they asked him, "How can it be?"
And Twig said, "I'll show you, come follow me."
They learned of his missions, and where he'd been to,
and watched in amazement as Twig squeezed on through.

They begged Twig to take them - he was wanted at last!
Twig had to think of a new plan... and fast!
"You use your strength to make the hole big."
So that's what they did before following Twig.

Twig wasn't lonely when out and about.
They passed Valerie vole with her very long snout,
Waved to Freddy frog, talked with Miss mole,
And told them about their escape through the hole.

They passed by Sid snail, gave a nod to each bird,
Who all thought that this sight was simply absurd!

Meanwhile the shepherd received a phone call:
Reports of some lambs on the loose - maybe all!
The sheepdog and shepherd ran out of the door,
To find their friend Twig... and twenty lambs more!

Returned to their field, the lambs were delighted,
Never before had they been so excited.
Exploring with Twig had been such a great day.
They now all saw him in a different way.

No one teased Twig now for being so small,
And always made sure he could play with them all.
Never a time was he lonely or glum
(Although he still enjoyed visits from shepherd mum).

Now Twig liked eating the grass all day long.
Stood with the flock - "This is where I belong."

Can you help Twig find his shepherd mum?

Finish

Start

Match these animals to their babies?

Dog - puppy

Sheep - lamb

Cat - kitten

Cow - calf

Test Your Knowledge

1. What will Twig grow up to be?

2. Who did Twig pass with a very long snout?

3. Who helped the shepherd find Twig?

4. What do lambs eat?

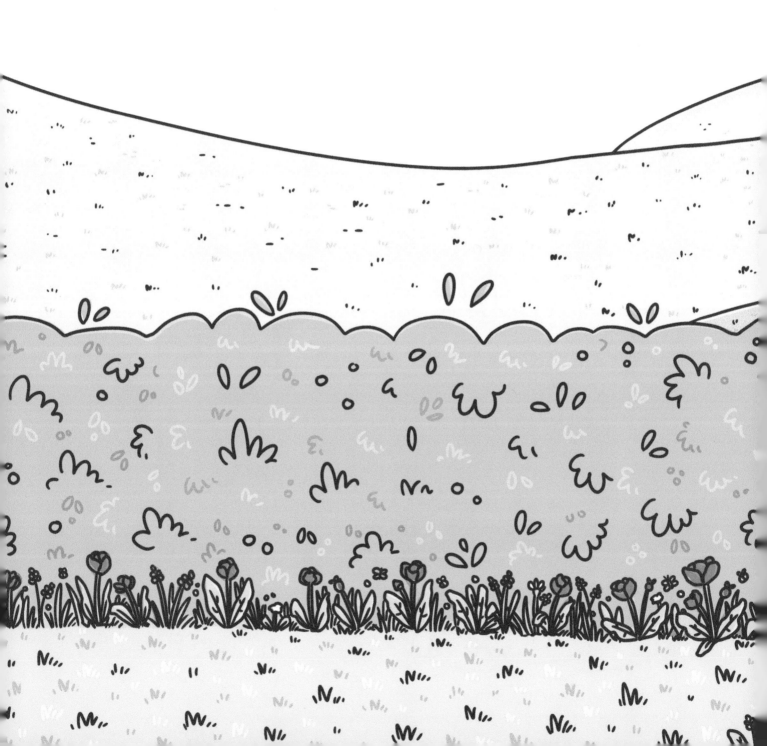

TRUE or FALSE?

1. Sheep have four stomachs.

2. Sheep live in the house with their shepherd.

3. Sheep have woolly coats that need to be sheared once a year.

4. Lambs are baby sheepdogs.

About the Author

As a mother of two boys, Lisa enjoys bedtime stories that are considered a treasured ritual, particularly rhyming, catchy picture books, where her boys marvel at the illustrations, get engrossed in the characters, and enjoy the rhythm of the poetry.

Lisa has always enjoyed writing poems and has written many for family and friends over the years to summarise a person, memory or experience.

Born and raised in Worcestershire, Lisa and her family moved from the town in which they grew up to the neighbouring countryside. Nestled within farmland, the love for farming soon took hold and so began their own hobby farm.

This new adventure has seen many big characters arise in the form of a small flock of sassy sheep, cheeky chickens, two charismatic cats (one of which thinks he is a sheepdog), three mischievous dogs, and some incredibly hysterical pet lambs (that are really dogs in disguise).

And of the four dogs in disguise, there is Twig, the sweetest, smallest orphan lamb that required hand rearing last year, and against all odds has thrived to this day. The sweet, strong, determined nature of this little lamb, that consistently found ways to find Lisa and her sheepdog, was remarkable. His strength of character is inspiring, as well as endearing, providing the perfect character and almost writing her first children's story for her. He really is an incredible little lamb, that has been a joy to watch develop and build his relationship with the other lambs and natural surroundings. This story encapsulates that and can bring some heart-warming inspiration to the bedtime read. Lisa is currently working on more characters to capture in a book for you!